This book is dedicated to my little brother, Jason.
I'll now happily pass on any sweater I've outgrown!

Dial Books for Young Readers
An imprint of Penguin Random House LLC, New York

First published in the United States of America by Dial Books for Young Readers,
an imprint of Penguin Random House LLC, 2022

Visit us online at penguinrandomhouse.com.

Library of Congress Cataloging-in-Publication Data is available.

Manufactured in China • ISBN 9780593461945
TOPL

10 9 8 7 6 5 4 3 2 1

Design by Lily Malcom
Text is set in Harimanu Dua and hand-lettered by Jessika von Innerebner

The art for this book was knitted together in Photoshop.

Olivia and her sweater do everything together.

If they part . . .

It's not for long.

But as Olivia grows, her favorite sweater doesn't.

Then one day, Olivia sees her
favorite sweater on . . .

(now it's a problem)

UNICORN BOARDS
It's time to pass it on, Olivia. We'll find you another one.
TIM'S ROOM KEEP OUT!

But Olivia doesn't want another sweater.
She wants HER sweater.

She vows to get it back!

Olivia just needs to find the right time to reclaim it.

At last, Olivia is reunited with her favorite sweater.

Then something catches her eye.

Olivia can't imagine letting go of her favorite sweater.

But maybe . . .

she can try.

Especially if passing this one down means it becomes . . .

Someone else's favorite.

Besides, her mom just gave her this cool new sweater.

And Olivia is really digging it.